THE CON MAN

Ramesh

Published by InkQuills Publishing House
www.inkquills.in

First Edition 2020

All Rights Reserved. Copyright © 2020

ISBN: 978-81-943552-7-4

CONTENT

Chapter – 1
An Ancient Fable: The Turtle

A turtle, banished from an elysian ocean, laid wilted on a terrain, exotic for him, somewhere far away from his home. Under the secure protection of his armour like a shell, he suspiciously inched his head out and regarded the grassy hedge labyrinth in which he was trapped in. For the turtle, albeit the maze was an amazingly bewildering topography of umpteen paths crisscrossing each other and running unceasingly, the visibility was limited to a thin path margined with tall hedge walls on either side. The path, rolled down a few yards and vanished at a curve around the corner and was bedded with damp green leaves and finely polished round cobbles that clattered to the slightest motion of his flap-like legs. Initially, for him, the solitary life between the tall hedges on which light-colored blooms and leaves sprang up copiously, seemed fascinating. "Magical" he said as a sudden upsurge of joy rouse his spirit and craned his neck out to study what his new abode looked like. The softness of the moist leaves and the shine of the cobbles gave him the impetus to move ahead and explore the unseen land. Swaying his short flap-like legs, the turtle dashed through the maze with an unquenchable eagerness to discover the new land. He nibbled on the hedge for food, amused himself with the clang of cobbles, treaded through the maze day in and day out. Days and nights passed. Intense summer beat upon the maze with its wrathful heat, the leaves dried up to bones, the turf wore a hue of pale yellow and the cobbles turned red hot iron. The lonely air of the labyrinth, which had once excited him began to reek. His solitude had now become a dark grotto that stifled him and drowned him to pensive melancholy. The wretched creature, immersed in utter despair, stood upright on his hint legs and prayed clapping his hands closed. "Oh Lord of the ocean, have you forgotten me, have mercy to show me a way out." Although his prayers were not answered for months, the turtle flipped through the forlorn loops of the never-ending labyrinth looking for a way out. During one such desolated dusk, when he was weeping inside his shell, his eyes suddenly caught sight of a gleam that emerged from the hedge wall. The uncanny glow emanated from the insides of the hedge that was towering a few yards in front of him. "The time has arrived for me to free myself" he shouted with joy and quickly dashed towards the glowing miracle which he was hopefully waiting for a long time. His heart thumped speedier as he approached the gleam and finally he rammed the hedge.

As soon as he hit the hedge wall, the leaves flapped open like a door and, with an abrupt plop swallowed the turtle into a different space. Soon a swoon overcame him. It was only after retrieving his consciousness that the turtle realized he was actually saved from the hedge labyrinth to live the rest of his life in a mirror labyrinth. However, his new home gave him a speck of respite, although for a short time. Even though cramped and confining, the mirror maze, because of its reflections, gave the illusion of a prodigious structure. Its insides were dark with a faint blue hue. Several mirror panels, fixed on all sides created illusory paths that stretched out to great length. The idea alone that his loneliness was resolved relieved the turtle, for he was always surrounded now by his reflections which imitated whatever he did. For one moment he studied their appearance on the mirror with surprise. All of them had stiff and bowed shells with deep stripes traversing and dividing it to definite grids. Their flap-like legs were extremely withered, as had his. Stretching out their lengthy and rugged neck they gaped at each other with their mournful eyes which sat at both sides of their angular face. The rampant turtle pleaded again "Oh lord of the mighty blue, I thank you for the mercy you've shown, nevertheless, have kindness to save me from this ordeal, perhaps sometime later even if not very soon." But he was appalled to find out the countless reflections of worshippers chanting the same prayer. Every one of his reflections copied his gestures and prayed exactly the way he did, instantly and invariably. This ludicrous mockery, prayers in vain and bitterness of monotonous similarity went on and on for days, weeks and months. Whenever the turtle stood on his hint legs to pray, the others also stood up. When he crawled inside to weep all the others followed and when he bellowed in agony so did the others.

With no hint of the passage of time, the turtle lived incarcerated inside the mirror maze spending many moons weeping and praying. He was so stifled by the imitating turtles that after a certain point, he entirely restricted himself of movements and began to sit motionless so that he wouldn't have to watch the reflections mock him. Sadly, even that did not ward off his plight as there was a myriad of turtles who sat idle and motionless when he did so.

At the birth of an unforeseen moment, an invisible palm of an unrevealed force touched the turtle's head and granted him a boon; that after 3000 full moons he will be blessed with the vision of a mermaid, Sea God's beloved daughter, who shall sanctify his soul and deliver him from the condemned life between reflections illusions and desolation.

Chapter – 2
The Con Man

"A venerable man."

"An ogre."

"His sense of beauty; a connoisseur!"

"Perhaps a nutter"

"An eccentric"

"An apostate"

"Of course, a benevolent man!"

I muttered these conjectures about Mr. Mann as I draped out on the neatly moved lawn in front of Elina's residence. The house was a reasonably significant construction built with unburnt clay bricks and polished wood, and had a veranda, fairly bedecked with porcelain pots that hung from solid brackets on the ceiling. With big rectangular windows and coned caps sitting at each corner of the angular roof, the double-storied structure that stood in the middle of a thicket-like land gave the impression of the most breathable dwelling one could ever build in the middle of a city strangled by multitudes and fume spitting vehicles. The front yard itself looked like a botanical garden with lines of lush bushes, dwarf trees and weeping willows that stood one after the other. Lying stretched out on the lawn and enjoying the soft warmth of sun,

I ruminated on what people said about Mr. Mann; mostly his victims and the rest the witnesses. Above my head, a jet plane that resembled a tin foil toy plane from that great height traversed the sky, leaving a string of white puffy smoke from its tiny butt hole. And after it rose to a certain height it vanished somewhere into the clouds that were beginning to invade the clear sky. Regardless of all those things that felt pleasant and comforting; the soothing trickle of wind that caressed the weeping willows, the bushes that snugged in the callow warmth of sun and velvety bed of lawn I was lying in, I was utterly dismayed as the rage towards Mr. Mann wound my nerves.

"Strange," I murmured as I saw a swarm of dark blue clouds floating in from the southwest. "How quickly has the sky changed her hue?" I reflected "an untrustworthy chameleon, with all its inherent crafty instincts." It didn't take much time for the clouds to huddle up and start their head to head battle; a few puerile ones engaged in a thunderous brawl and busted themselves, landing the first patter of rain on my face. I quickly pressed both my arms behind my head, bent my legs close to the torso and with a forceful leap sprang up stably on both my feet; all in one motion and paced towards the veranda with palms covering my hair from soaking.

"Strange!" I uttered in a contemptuous tone as I felt vexed at the unprecedented weather tantrums she had been showing these days. I shadowed my eyes with my hand and peered at the sky to inspect whether there was some whimsical elf lurking behind the clouds, enchanting the earth under his magical spells. The rain lashed down for some more time and then slowly retreated. It was only after the rain subsided that I heard the whisper that slowly rose from the other side of the window. From the sweetness of the voice it was over that it was of a female. The lady spoke so fretfully that she jittered almost throughout the conversation. Straining my ears, I stood quietly at the veranda, listening to the conversation and when the lady hung up the phone, I knocked on the door. There was no response for some time although I knew the lady was somewhere inside. I thought of giving it a second try and knocked again. "Is there someone inside?" I asked by the end of three knocks, loudly enough for my voice to pass through the closed windows and reach the lady's ears. Even my second attempt died in vain. "Either the lady must have left through the rear door or something creepy must have happened to her" I thought. The glass panes of the window were smudged from spray of the recent rain and hence did not reveal much of the interior. So I dighted up the droplets from the glass and blinkered my eyes with my palms so as to peek in and have a better view of the insides. There was no trace of anyone inside the cozy interiors of the house. Abruptly, a cold shudder passed down my spine as a pair of dark, thick lashed eyes bobbed up and stood right in front of my nose with only the glass pane dividing them from mine. Appalled by that uncanny encounter, the girl bounded a few steps back and slunk down to a chair with both her palms covering her charming face.

"Are you alright, my love?" I asked the girl, unsure if she had heard my voice. Although I was aware of the urgency of revealing my whereabouts to the girl and soothing her down, I didn't even attempt because I knew it would be an utterly useless effort from my part to talk to her before she could at the least breath normally. So I waited at the veranda and left her to calm herself down. After a couple of minutes, while I was studying the intricate designs of the mosaicked floor, the girl came and stood near the window with a timid, unconfident expression on her face. For a brief time, she faltered indecisively whether to open the window or not. But finally having gathered courage she unfastened the clasp and opened the window partly.

"I apologize my dear" I said, "I must say that I pose no threat to you and I am here just to exchange a few words with my friend Elina." Although my words seemed to have alleviated her fear to an extent; from her gestures it was evident that she wasn't convinced enough to open the front door to let me in.

"Have you got an appointment sir?" she stammered doubtfully.

"No. I haven't." I answered her briskly and with a blithe expression on my face. Her behavior was so hysterical that metaphorically, she seemed like a caged parrot, petrified by the terrifying sight of a rapacious cat waiting patiently for that vicious moment to lunge at her. She quickly dialed her phone again and rang up someone, which must have been Elina. She covered her mouthpiece and murmured over the phone, casting furtive glances at me through the corner of her eyes to reassure her safety. It was only when I heard the conversation I realized that her watchful eyes had been spying me from the time I entered the property. But I don't blame her for considering me as an ominous stranger.

When a trespasser invades your property, when he sprawls out nonchalantly on the lawn, stomps through the façade hissing and grumbling words that are nonsensical to you, things would get on anybody's nerves. And specially if it's a psychiatrist's residence for that matter, the one like Elina's, people would be petrified to black icy rock.

"I beg your pardon sir," she said "Elina would return only in an hour. Please have the patience to wait or maybe we can fix another appointment." she said timidly and slid in a newspaper through the rails of the window, for me to read in case I chose to wait.

"That's alright darling. I can wait" I replied in a soft voice. But before I could speak further she hurried off to the insides and disappeared. Throwing the paper on the dwarf tea table and I started pacing the length of the veranda. Down a few steps, a path nearly four feet wide, paved with flat stones, lined with dwarf bushes on both of its sides, ran down till the front gate, dividing the lush front yard. A short while of walk called up in me the thoughts about Mann. I pitied those poor people who felt victims to his treacherous plays. As the episodes of his victims flashed through my head, I unconsciously began to speak to myself again. Many called him a wise man, a righteous man and there were many who scorned him as a brute. Some contrasted this judgement saying he was just a nutter. Some others lauded him as a non-conformist. But as far as I was concerned, of all that I know about him he was nothing more than a con man, a deceiver of the first order.

Chapter – 3
The Wait

Two pensive hours went by. The sky stretched out a bright veil over the town and the sun beat upon the earth so fiercely that the dampness left by the rain seemed like a bygone memory. Moment after moment, the atmosphere grew into a blazing furnace as if the sun was purging all its fury upon the all forbearing earth before it began its descend from the sky.

I had a quick glance at my watch that laid wilted around my wrist and found that Elina had apparently taken more time than what the girl had said. Nevertheless, I was unflinching on meeting Elina. No matter how much time it took, I decided to wait till she returned and to seek help from her to free me of these strangling thoughts. I sank to a wooden chair on the veranda and waited for half-hour more before I dozed off to a short nap. Later, a rough squeal of the gate woke me up from the dream. I cast a quick glance around the garden and found the person I had been waiting for all the while. Closing the gate behind her, Elina was walking hastily through the thin stone strewn path that rolled down the lawn. I regarded her from tip to toe. Her whole demeanor had changed over the last six years. She wore a short gown. Her widened hips had filled the breadth of the wear and there were hints of her flabbier loins.

Her ruddy cheeks looked fleshier. Yet the charisma that flooded her face still lingered on. The sheer glance of that beautiful female who was once my bosom mate refreshed my eyes and drew my mind back to the musty smelling aisles of the university library. It was there that our friendship had budded and blossomed.

As I remember, at that time I had just turned twenty-three and Elina had been in her late twenties. Those were days when I was living the skint life of a student, a student of psychology. Elina happened to visit our department as a guest speaker. I can still recollect the image of that statuesque, well-mannered lady and her eloquent talk on the subject "Expressions of the first man." Later that evening, after the talk, I stalked her to the university library where she had been walking along the long aisles, scanning the long racks of books, and made acquaintance. Elina visited the university time and again and in the freshness of our newborn relation, we travelled together, exchanged new books that we stumbled upon, loitered at the university café, fell out over arguments, reconciled again, explored and experienced new ways of savoring earthly pleasures, 'creative engagement' as I would call it. This went on and on till I graduated from the university. Years after we parted, when we used to communicate through letters, she had written to me that she was intrigued by an abstract quality which had drawn her closer to me.

The gradual growth of our passion and its culmination happened at a certain phase of life, during which I, as a person, was wholly raw and rugged. Then I was a naïve, explorative swain with no façade, no intention of leaving impression on others and no desire of hanging on to relations which I considered mundane. Hence, I bluntly confronted everything and everyone who was discordant with my set of beliefs. It was during this phase that she made an appearance in my life with all her differences and imperfections. All through our relation, these disagreements and differences rubbed coarsely against each other and created intense friction. We argued intensely, disputed intensely and fought intensely but was still vehemently in love. I often pondered if such a relation would be possible in the later part of our lives where we would resort to adjustments instead of facing it head-on and smoothening out the sharp edges of our characters. Because of this coarse evolution, our deep relation remained perennial in the hidden corners of our hearts, even though we had to part at a certain point in time. And because of this, even after a long-standing silence and separation, we could speak and connect with the same freshness and passion.

While years passed like minutes, frivolously and uninterruptedly, I spent most of my time in buses, trains and bikes, traversing the country while Elina worked fervently and resolutely on her dream of becoming a psychiatrist. Even though I wrote to her occasionally, never did I know that our paths would converge again at a point when I was badly in need.

A smile of surprise lit up Elina's face as her shining eyes caught sight of me.

"Was that you? Where on earth were you, my friend? Haven't heard from you for quite some time? Were you the stranger who gave Rosa a taste of terror?" She paused after a long string of questions. The girl appeared again by the window but this time she wore a grin on her face.

"Rosa, this is my dearest friend. Being a student of phycology once, he is an effing madcap like myself," said Elina with a slight inclination of her head and both the ladies burst out laughing at once.

"By the way, this young lady here is my caretaker. The most efficient, especially when dealing with clients" standing behind the window Rosa grinned sheepishly as Elina teased her.

When Elina raved about me and our good old days to the caretaker, unceasingly, all I did was smile and acknowledge everything she said until I found the right moment of silence where I could smoothly chip in the purpose of my visit. And when such a moment of silence finally arrived, "Elina I need to speak to in private, it's important" I said shifting my glance furtively to the care taker who was listening to us.

"Yes, yes. Sure." Elina replied "but beforehand let me quickly freshen up myself" and rubbing out the tiny drops of sweat that blossomed on her glossy forehead she gently pushed open the front door. Rosa neared the door and stood there with a smile broader than before and showed gestures which indicated that she had acquainted to my presence. Elina suggested that it's better to talk in her private study and therefore instructed Rosa to get me settled there. Giving me a cheerful nudge, the young lady conducted me through a dimly lit passage and opened a door that stood at the far end of the hallway. The door opened to an impressive interior. A spacious cube-shaped room with dark blue cushioned chairs and voluminous settees arranged on three of its sides. The floor was mosaicked light blue and almost at the centre of the room stood a six legged wood topped table on which perched quite a good collection of antiques and souvenirs and a stack of newly delivered books that looked fresh in its transparent wrap. A reading lamp quartered one corner of the table, stooping its sleek thin neck and overlooking its polished surface. From its yawning mouth spewed out a pale yellow flash on to the table top. The room did not have a fourth wall, instead, facing the door, stood a massive shelf with an impressive collection of books and case files sectionalized neatly with their spine facing outward. I quickly swept my eyes back and forth through the shelf and read the titles which were printed on the books. Writers, poets, philosophers and her cases, all on the same boat. However, unlike the abundantly aerated house, the room barely had any windows except for a line of ventilation holes which were hollowed out from top part of the wall.

"Take a seat, if you please" Rosa spoke softly "and if you need me for anything, don't hesitate." she pointed her finger to a tiny red button that bulged out of the wall, just above the telephone table, like a waxed pimple.

"Surely, I would let you know, cheers" I replied with a light smile. The girl wheeled around swirling her short skirt and walked off gently closing the door behind her. I reclined slowly and comfortably to the couch entwining my hands behind my head on the head rest, studying the lavishly decorated room at the same time. "Well, this place is quite elegant, just being in it

A dead, noiseless moment ensued. Only the pitiful, faint sputters and crackles of the burning cigarette flakes, as the fire devoured it, was heard. Elina took another drag and blew wreaths of smoke up in the air. With a smile she said "Fair enough, we shall figure out. Don't be worried."

A shine of confidence gleamed in my eyes as I heard those words of countenance. Her beautiful eyes rested sternly and attentively on me. For an instance my eyes interlocked with hers and we sat face to face gazing at each other, like in our youthful days, with our caring eyes studying each other.

I must say I was a true aesthete of eyes. For I have seen many soulful spheres on many faces, mostly found in unexpected places or people or even animals; on the sludgy alleys of the slums, inside the sweat reeking bedchambers of bawdy houses, or on some of those rapacious ravens that you see on the river banks (picking on half scorched human corpse). All beautiful and bewitching. But for me, nothing held a candle to Elina's pair of large almonds, her gleaming black pupils and curly lashes that shuttered and opened lightly and leisurely. Sometimes I felt as if her sharp glances were ransacking my soul.

"All right, alright. Perhaps we should start discussing things then" she said as she propped back slowly against the back rest and gave me a merry wink, having understood the passion with which I was admiring her eyes.

Chapter – 4
The Rebel

Elina reached out for the ashtray. Holding it in her hand she took a few more drags and tipped the ash. The turtle with welled up eyes captured my attention again. I went completely mindless. Along with the strange feeling that the picture gave me, of which I didn't know what to make of, I also pondered over a way to unfold Mr. Mann's story. Even that seemed like a daunting task. I was utterly befuddled. Meanwhile, Elina who was dissecting and scrutinizing my body language all the while, as soon as she figured out my unearthly interaction with the magazine, brought her painted nails over the face page and tapped lightly on it.

"How are we?" she broke the silence.

"I…" I paused "I have no clue about how to put this across, things seem to be much more complex than they were" I said shifting my glance from the magazine to the floor. My mind aimlessly wandered through the shady aisles of my memory.

"That's perfectly fine, there must be some way for sure" she assuaged my bewilderment "where was it that you encountered him lately? I am interested to learn about that. May be that may help us decide the course of our conversation."

How we begin or where we begin was not of much significance as far as I was concerned, for me it was all about where we ended and how we ended. So I began.

"I first stumbled across him at the golf club where an informal gathering, conducted by some activists, was being held." I paused "But first of all you must know about Mr. Chloe, the host of the gathering. Mrs. Chloe, popularly known as 'The Mother', was an active ecologist as well as a renowned author. At the age of 35 she abandoned her daily job and turned a staunch environmentalist after she confronted the absurdity of her 'unproductive existence', as she had written in her memoir. Subsequently, she spent almost a year in a jungle, in the south-east of Asia, with the primitive tribes and learned fervently about the plant life and vegetation of the tribal village. Later Chloe, her husband and three other friends materialized their long- desired dream of setting up a nature conservative club and started off by constructing model forests in cities; what they called urban afforestation. A good part of her day was spent on educating communities about the benefits of planting trees and rest of the time was invested for her writing".

I recalled whatever I had learned from her book "The Pristine valley; A memoir".

"The internal matters regarding their nature club was kept in high secrecy and no new comers were allowed to the join or even associate in the club's activities. In Chloe's words, things were more effective and quick when worked out by a compact team. Although, the organization, in its sheer size, did not beef up with new entrants, its fame grew so rampantly that after a span of two years they became the busiest forest makers, moving like nomads from one city to other and from there to another".

In this one-sided conversation, I methodically narrated all what I had learned about Chloe and the organization through my research. Dwelling into the unknown, especially when it holds a potential danger, was almost like a ritual for me. Being oblivious meant being insecure and hence I felt it almost incumbent on me to investigate even on smaller issues that hooked my attention. And as far as the case of Con man was concerned, it had deprived me of sleep for days.

"Now let me tell you something that 'the mother' had not written and would not want to write." I carried on. "The gathering at the golf club as planned by Chole was a pivotal decision which would have strengthened the organization drastically, if implemented. Finance would have gushed in abundantly, Chloe and her team's fortune would have changed for the best. Chloe, besides her 'noble humane quality', also bore a shrewd business acumen which her stout husband or anybody in her team for that matter, lacked. That could have been the plausible reason to why she, at her sole discretion, chose to open up the organization's gate for outsiders after their clientele and her readers expanded. She would have definitely reconsidered what she had written and spoken about working in short team and its effectiveness. Chloe wasn't focusing on the mediocre people whom you see on the street. But her real intent was to influence the elite youth and acquire their countenance as she deemed them as a category which could bring about real change.

At the Golf club the congregation was about to commence, velvety carpets with floral designs were rolled out. The meeting room was opulently lit with golden yellow light. The cozy sofas where being occupied one after another by the invitees who arrived in their flashy cars. Meanwhile, at the entrance, the steward boy had given a thumbs up for Mr. Mann to enter. He threaded nonchalantly through the half occupied room and threw himself on a couch that sat in an isolated corner of the hall. He wore a dull chequered shirt and black saggy trousers which laid wilted till his feet. A pair of round, thick lenses that he wore magnified his pensive eyes and gave them a gleam of ethereal brilliance. The naïve steward boy might have had succumbed to his artifice, as had the others in the hall. They all presumed that he had come on behalf of the other party. Of all the invitees that turned up the most distinguished were two brothers Hani and Omar, sons and heirs of a media mogul. Despite being siblings, Hani and Omar had only very few attributes in common. Hani was tall, slim and had a coarse resolute face. Omar, on the other hand, was short and squat. He carried an elegance smile on his plump face which always left a pleasant impression on the people he met. Regardless of all the odds and contradictions, the brothers had a warm understanding of each other which helped them operate smoothly like two cogwheels. But there was one thing which fascinated both of them alike; Sky watching".

Like a rolling dice that has suddenly come to repose I paused and looked at Elina. A graphite pencil had replaced the cigarette now. Twiddling the pencil between her fingers, she was making metal notes of my body language and my narration.

I continued by imitating Chloe "Yes folks. thank you for turning up. We are truly overwhelmed by the ardour and sprit you have shown… We are delighted that we could find the right people who would take our campaign to success'. Chloe said in a rhetoric voice and enthroned herself into a voluminous armchair while her husband and partners took position on both sides of the chair. All of them were uniformly garbed in pale- green t-shirts that bore the name of their club. Chloe, the shortest of them all, had bobbed hair streaked with faint strands of grey and her thin lips painted red to highlight its perfect bow. Each sentence that escaped her mouth was so carefully choreographed with rise and falls that sometime later everybody was engrossed in her voice that filled the hall. She started off with a snippet of their organization and their activities and moved on swiftly to expounding the purpose of the gathering. She vehemently spoke about the need of nature conservation and ruthlessly condemned poaching and clear-cutting. Her eyes were ablaze with rage when she spoke about the rate at which our oceans were being littered and her voice quavered when she poetically voiced the lament of mother earth. Sometimes she perturbed the listens with the unprecedented accounts of natural disasters exposed the vulnerability of human species. 'Till the arid blooms' she commanded in her shrilly voice. Time and again, a wave of applause passed through the audience drowning her solitary talk. At a certain point she called everyone's attentions to a big fat book that had been sitting, all through the talk, on the glass topped table beside her. The book had umpteen pages and was quite fat for her stubby palms to hold. To pen that sort of book, single-handedly, would have definitely taken at least 3 years of inexorable commitment. It could possibly be a fruit of team work as well. Anyways, she heaved the book with both her hands, turned the front towards the audience and swayed it so that all could see. 'WHO ARE WE WAITING FOR? A SORCERER?' read the title. The shortest of those who occupied the back seats curiously lifted their butt by two inches from the chair to look. This book was Chloe's latest release. If everything had come along as Chloe had plotted, her new book release would have been a massive event and hence would have her readers would have proliferated exponentially. All the invitees, except the brothers, a young man in blue blazer and a woman in a black sheath dress who sat beside him, were quite intrigued by Chloe's rhetoric and the book. A shade of infectious suspicion flashed through the young man's face and got passed on to the lady's. Hani's and Omar's minds were wandering somewhere else. All the while when Chloe spoke, they were restlessly murmuring to each other and turning back to look at Mr. Mann who sat silently and thoughtful in an unnoticed corner. 'Isn't that him?' asked Hani to his brother in low voice and cocked his ears for the reply. It was at that moment that Mr. Mann opened his mouth to speak".

Chapter – 5
Vicious Mouth

"'Mrs. Chloe' the Con Man called out loudly and sternly 'I must say… I am taken aback by the exceptional marketing expertise you have shown' he heaved a sneer on his face as her spoke. 'But how pitiful that you unceasingly talk about your love for nature, its lamentations, tears, agony and all such big things while you hold an effing fat book in your hand, which is nothing but the flesh of those trees you were taking about a minute ago. Are you not ashamed?'. The hall drowned into stark silence as Mr. Mann paused. Chloe's face turned scarlet and the thick air of embarrassment stifled her. Meanwhile, goaded by Mr. Mann's unnecessary remarks, her husband, a stout man with solid bones, was beginning to approach Mr. Mann in an attempt to grab him by his neck and throw him out, but his attempt was thwarted promptly by Chloe. Some invitees gazed at each other in confusion, some turned their head half way around and looked at corner where Mann sat. The suspicious gentleman and the lady huddled up in an aloof corner and murmured something under their breath. Mann's censure didn't stop there and he went on 'Had you not written that book, Mrs. Chloe, the earth would have been a bit a greener. You are nothing less than a shameless money grubber. And about these docile swines standing off in your shadow, devil gives a damn!'. Mann's words rumbled across the hall. Stung by the unmerited insult and provocation, Chloe's husband growled like a rabid dog and tightened his fist. If it had not been for his prudent wife, he would have pounced at Mr. Mann and pulled out his streaming guts. But unstirred by the ruffle, the brothers were brooding over Mann, taking conspicuous glances at him and trying to recollect."

"After a short time, the young lady in the black sheath dress stepped forward and expressed her gentle refusal. 'Mrs. Chloe, I appreciate your efforts to make this campaign happen and I am happy about your invitation. However, I am having second thoughts. If I may say, with no disrespect, I find a point in what that man said. I must apologize, I am stepping back' she said looking for Mann, but he had already reached the exit. The invitees who were mindlessly gazing at each other started muttering and discussing. Some of the potential investors sprang up from their seat, wheeled around resolutely and walked out through the door, having lost their interest. And for Chloe and her team, never did it occur that anything of this sort would devastate their plans. Never before had she been made such an imbecile before her audience. Her face reddened with embarrassment and rage. For the twin brothers, it was shocking to finally identify the loud- mouthed Mann as the same person whom they had seen at the Cliff with Evan, their dear companion and a sky watch maniac."

""That's him, believe me brother. It is the same brute who was with Evan at the Ridge' Omar grumbled to his brother with welled up eyes. With pain and anger simmering inside them, the brothers resolutely decided to glean the whereabouts of Mr. Mann no matter what it costed and hold him legally responsible for what he had done to Evan".

Chapter – 6
The Hide

"Turns out this guy, Mann, is a gloom-monger" Elina sniggered, vexed by the pernicious remarks made by Mann that seemed absurd and irrational to her. "Mrs. Chloe is a staunch activist. I have long heard of her and her contributions. Unarguably a stalwart. Moreover, money making doesn't makes you a terrible sinner, does it? Nothing can happen without material aid, which is nothing but money?". She defied Mr. Mann stubbornly. But I genuinely doubt whether she could decipher the real meaning of conman's words as effective as the lady in the Black sheath cloth.

"Of course, what you said may sound real for a level- headed human. But only if you burrow in and extract the real essence of his words…" I confronted Elina straight out for her poor judgement and she felt indignant for being belittled as a single-layered thinker. Without giving room for her to counter her arguments and looking straight into her narrowed eyes I continued. "All what Mr. Mann did was to wait patiently for Mrs. Chloe to mould a beautiful, glossy wax candle so that he could set light on its head and watch it melt under its own heat." I articulated in a single breath, chewing each word with content before escaped my lips.

For a moment, Elina's eyes flitted around the books on the wooden shelf. "Never can a loving son write about the glory and sanctity of motherhood with the ink of his mother's blood and quills made of her bones. For a true son know he is nothing but his mother" I said pausing and asserting each word with utmost clarity.

Now Elina was drowning into a muddle. She extracted another cigarette from the case and lit it before it's butt touched her lips. "I am surprised that you are advocating Mr. Mann now. As far I know that wasn't your purpose, at least when we began. Is that you who got derailed or is it I who went wrong?" She summoned an embarrassing smile, lowered her head and pressed her forehead.

"Neither of us" I said "Neither of us are wrong nor am I advocating Mr. Mann. All I behold is the light in his words. For me he is a lightless man, but he might reflect. His way with words, while he spoke at the club, was such that its mere purpose was to impress any listener and turn them vulnerable to misjudge him as a maverick, perhaps an altruistic man or even as a staunch environmentalist who debunks all pretentious swindlers- But only if they had not caught him at 'HIDE', living it up with a group of drummers, spending day hours in their workshops; in the middle of wood shavings and wood splinters, carpentering the best of djembe shells, drying animal hides for the skin and relishing his earthly moments to its core… like Zorba". For a brief moment my eyes travelled over to the left top cabin of the book shelf, half empty with the remaining books laying back on each other.

"Very well. then enlighten me with more of this mad man's tales" said Elina in a low whisper and drew my attention back to her grinning face. I felt as if she had attuned to the course of my emotions. I felt we were like contrasting petals of a two petal- flower, wafting together in an alternate stream of breeze.

"Hide" I began "was a drummers joint that sat inside a mahogany forest located in the suburbs of 'THE CITY'. A community of drummers- precisely those quirky, free spirited, non-conformist, well- educated hippies who censured the main stream city dwellers and the irreconcilable fissure they had with the sheer natural state of human existence."

"Initially HIDE was an encampment conceptualised by a dozen musicians, both men and women, who decided to abandon the CITY and trekked the forest to establish a new free society where they could live organically. They clear-felled a portion of the mahogany forest and constructed a few shepherd huts using the fallen trees. They poached wild buffalos for meat and parched its hide for djembe skins. They spent their daytime hunting and enjoying the green and by dusk they huddled near their dwellings and ravished in music. Later after months, when a wild photojournalist on one of his expeditions, happened to pass by the HIDE flashed a few snippets, bringing their stories to the public attention henceforth. Sooner the HIDE community swelled up with new incomers and the HIDE djembes gained a remarkable prominence in the market. The encampment which was just a huddle of 5 shepherd huts at first, expanded to 10, then to 20 and by the time the con man arrived at the HIDE it had turned into a small village with high- clearance shacks, huts, tends for visitors, small community halls and food stalls. Quite soon a pillar in the shape of an obelisk was planted at the centre of the tiny settlement and a wooden hoarding with 'HIDE' etched on it, was clamped to its top. At night they kindled fire woods and lost themselves in their music. Drum beats resonated across the thicket like throbs of the wild and when the day broke they fell more tree and made djembes and other percussions. A narrow unpaved road through which only motor bikes and working animals could pass was cleared out through the thicket to transport their merchandise. Vested interest obscured in whatever they embarked. Even though they had all means to build a proper road to transport their product, the idea of narrow, unpaved path was put forth to show their little interest in forging a connection with THE CITY and despite the unforeseen development, they doggedly kept their life untainted from the rules, convictions and dogmas that shackled the city dwellers. They never complied with a pre-set routine for anything they undertook, women and men coupled very often with mutual consent. Many of them, at their own will and discretion walked around naked and the practice was adopted by yet many, regardless of their age. Eventually, at the HIDE, physical appearance took a back seat. And unlike THE CITY where meticulously dressed men and women fornicated in rented lodges and teenagers snogged amorously behind the abandoned ranches and grandpas were still in tussle to contain their lust, at the HIDE penis driven love was waning."

I looked at Elina. With her motionless eyes glued to mine and her head tilted slightly towards her right shoulder, she was pondering, perhaps building a HIDE in her mind with her thoughts. I decided to carry on before her mind trudged back from the HIDE.

"Mann appeared at the HIDE after the first downpour of that year's monsoon. Drenched in the torrential rain, the thicket stood dark and chilled. Occasionally a squall would pass through the thicket and sweep the damp foliage westwards. Mr. Mann, when he emerged at the commune had long wiry hair that flowed down to his shoulders and lower part of his face covered with thick facial hair that shined brown in the sun shine. He always walked around half naked in his micro-trunks, exposing his lush body hair that blanketed his powerful chest. His shoulders were broad, his body was shredded and he was a man of solid bone. Moreover, his swollen calves with defined muscles added on to his wildness. The thick glasses he wore at the Golf club was now removed to reveal his hawk-eyes"

As I was explaining, I abruptly felt an urge to puff on a couple of smoke. I leaned towards the table and walked my fingers towards the cigarette case. Elina tossed the lighter on to my lap all at once. I pulled out a cigarette and the fragrant flavour of clove pervaded my mouth immediately.

"No one was ever admitted or denied entry to the HIDE" I continued, blowing out thick billow of smoke as I spoke "One had to gel with the commune and gradually evolve his fellowship. That could be one reason why most of the zealous entrants, even though they bore similar thoughts, didn't stay for long. Because nobody was there to receive them, provide them a quick tour and give them a feeling of acceptance. Many might have got befuddled about organic functioning of the system and might have felt immense desolation inside the commune. Mann raised his arch tent near the workshop, aside a reasonably big shepherd hut which had a high land clearance that would easily allow an adult man to crawl through. All his bearings were piled up at one corner of the tent and essential cooking apparatus were stuffed in a sack and left outside. A foldable pocket knife, with irregular grooves on one side and sharply grinded blade on the other, always laid in his pocket. It didn't take Mann, a long time to attune to the life at HIDE. The foremost engagement with the drummers during the first few days was at the workshop where he lent hands to help them heave heavy rolls of wood from the forest for sculpting djembe frames. Some days he occupied himself with helping them shave the wood and pull the ropes to tune the skin. He had wisely chosen the site for his lodging so as to be at the workshop most of the time and forge bond with the members. At night he appeared at the fire camp and displayed the dexterity of his fingers on drums. Whenever he laid hands on the tightly toned djembe, all the others were wallowed in until his supple fingers paused. "Rattle of snake" they lauded his crisp single stroke rolls. His mastery was not just confined to drumming; he also possessed brilliant skills in hunting, precisely reptilian hunting."

"Did you say reptilian hunting?" asked Elina with a frown of disgust "sounds ridiculous for a man who gushed so emotionally about nature".

"I see… now you are getting it right" I replied and recalled a memory. "you know… once the Hide members (Hiders, as they were known) were inside the forest, obscuring behind the boughs and bushes, waiting silently for the right moment to fire down a solitary deer which was grazing in the grassy land of the forest. Everyone sharpened their focus and stood breathless. Abruptly, an earth shaking bang sent the deer scrambling away. All the eyes instantly went down to Mann who was lying on the ground, gripping a monitor lizard by its tail. The lizard was plump and dark, and its leathery skin looked weathered and coarse. The spiteful monster writhed violently as Mann tightened his clench. Forming a circle around the wild duel, the Hiders beheld the devilish fury with which the man consummated the kill; he clumsily dug out the knife from his pocket, dragged the lizard closer, sank the sharp knife to its neck and twisted it from side to side till the creature laid motionless.

It was only after a few days, when they huddled up as usual, for the fire camp, that they realised the reason why Mann had hunted the lizard. With him, wrapped in a light brown rag, came an instrument that was exotic for them. "Khanjira" Mann called it. (Khanjira, a round Indian hand drum made by stretching out dried lizard skin on a thick wooden ring, the size of a flattened palm.) 'Expressions are peerless. Nothing comes close to it'. He said about the tiny hand drum and brought it closer to his ears. Giving it a bouncy tap near its rim he closed his eyes to listen to its resonant plop. He then sat to one corner of a wooden bench and recollected his experience where he had witnessed a mammoth- sized elephant, wild and dark, wandering alone thought the forest. Now this was something which Mann enjoyed the most during their late night gathering. He loved the way hiders hung to his words when he crafted a story and presented it in unison with the rhythm"

"This time the tale was that of an elephant, a mad beast! An elephant, bathed in raven black, strayed from the herd roved all along the length and breadth of the forest seeking a mate. His madness and lust oozed down from both sides of the elephant's large formidable head like thick syrup. Powerfully rocking his head in frustration, he slapped his enormous ears against his own back. The sick-sweet smell sweet smell of blood always surrounded him. One wild moment, in an upsurge of fury, the portentous creature charged against a solid bough and thrashed it repeatedly with its head and tusk. The bough was so strong that one of his tusk burst off in the second strike. But the enraged animal did not give up and swung his head with more and more power and pounded the bough till it broke.' Mann fell silent for a moment, cupped his hands on the Khanjira and began drumming out a slow paced rhythm; a sequence of heavy slaps and thuds although slow. Entangled in resounding booms came a crisp roll of his fingers. One of the eldest of the hiders, who was absorbed in the rhythmic narration, looked into the dark thicket and saw the mad mammoth. For him the imaginary animal had begun to scratch its wobbly trunk against the rough bough. Step by step the rhythm climbed to a speedier pace and then soared to remarkable pace with beats, off beats and resonant gulps. The subtle interplay of the elephant's tale and Khanjira beats enraptured the hiders and they sat completely immersed in the rendition. This went on until the crack of the bough was heard. For a few seconds that ensued, only the puff and pant of the cold night breeze and the alternate whisper and crackling of burning fire woods were heard. The elder man paced to his shack, brought out his melodica and began pierced the breeze with an exhilarating tune. Mann fortified the music with perfect drum beats. Some half- naked women rose from the ground clapping their hands, lifted their chin, rolled back their eyes and began to shake along with the tune before their light movements gradually grew into strange jumps and whirls. They stepped in circles around the flamboyant old man and Mann.

Men and women with Djembes and ukuleles flew in from different directions. In the acme of that exuberant night, HIDE quaffed the sweet nectar of music till the first beam of daylight blessed them with a happy sleep"

"Day after Day, night after night, Mann's charm enraptured the Hiders. Nubile females admired him and loved to saunter with him through the damp woods. They loved to snug in the warmth of his powerful hairy chest. Hiders proliferated drum varieties by extracting knowledge from his profound experiences. "Globetrotter" they acknowledged him in their conversations. Each day, when the night fell, they willingly melted to one spirit and ambled along the narrow edge of the risky ridge that Mann created with his joyful and sorrowful rhythm. At daybreak they went home with content and gratitude for him. Sometimes their music soared to the dizzy heights of joy and sometimes winged down to the valley of tears. Some nights, after certain mental thresholds, howls and shouts of liberation accompanied with melodica, djembes and Conges rose in the air. Tears streamed down Mann's rough-featured face at times. Once a young girl, while snogging in the woods, caressed his hair and asked him why he was so passionate and happy in every single thing that he undertook. 'Each day buds as a tiny bubble and bursts as a bigger bubble by the nightfall, I am not interested whether it bursts with a scent or stench. All that makes me happy is the fact that it bursts'. He breathed his words into her ears and nuzzled his face to her neck. Slowly and inconspicuously, HIDE was transforming into a cult. Their fascination for Mann grew till a point where they constructed for him, the first tree hut on a tall tree high enough to watch over the whole of their settlement. But Con Man vanished the next night, bursting like a big bubble and disappearing for ever".

"But, let me put forth a genuine doubt". Elina asked suspiciously.

"You may… please" I assured her of my transparency.

"How do you know all these happenings?" Elina immediately hurled a genuine question which provoked me for some oblivious reason.

"Of course, brain box. I know. Otherwise how could I tell you about all what happened!?" I yelled bitterly at Elina as I resented her suspicion.

"Calm down love. I was just wondering" Elina tried to soothe me down "I am surprised at the painstaking attention you give to each detail. Strange, I must say. Who is he for you?".

Elina's words landed like a hefty blow and for some reason gave me flashes of that turtle and those two sibyls who had kept wagging their fingers at me. "Who is he for me?" I kept murmuring it over and over again like a possessed lunatic. My face grew pale like the chalky face of a dead man. I felt my nerves winding my soul like a python, my mouth dried out and a sort of heaviness in my head plunged me to a state of delirium. Pressing my temples tightly with my fingers I lowered my head. Even a quick glance at the wall made me dizzy as they seemed to ripple.

"Aaaa yaaoo ayyytttt" a wobbly, unearthly sound that set forth from Elina's mouth reached my ears like a rumble and at once the voice of boot whacks from a distance emerged piercing the rumble. The whacks were growing louder and louder as if it were stomping towards me. Given the exorbitant rate at which the boot whacks grew, I was terrified if it would louden to a point where my ear drums would explode. Three earth shaking bangs reverberated the door. Petrified, I rolled up over on the sofa, with my eyes palms guarding my nape and forearms concealing my ears. Transfixed in the petrified emotional state, I tightly shut my eyes to cut off everything outside. In a short while Elina gave me a shot of tranquiliser and helped me recuperate. However, an annoying heaviness restrained me from making active movements. I laid wilted on the couch like a loose cloth, with all my energy dissipated. It was only after sometime, when Elina told me it was actually Rosa who knocked on the door, that I opened my eyes. Rosa had come to serve us tea.

"Hope you are better now?" Elina spoke in a gentle voice as she placed her tender palm on my head.

"Yes. Feeling much better" I mumbled.

"Let's go out and refresh our mind. breath some fresh air and you will be back to normal" said Elina.

"Yes" I said desperately, as though happy for the arrival of the long awaited moment to free myself from some sort of confinement. I stumbled over to the door. Elina came to my side, threw her arms around my shoulders and drew me to her warmth. While we were heading to the back yard, she slid her hands through my collar and rubbed my back. Either it must have been a gesture of affection or it must have been her clever move to check whether I had bodily hair like Mr. Mann. Anyways. As soon as we reached the rear door, Elina drew the hasp and pulled the wooden door open. And seeing the backyard, I was surprised to know the pace at which time had passed. Now the sky was inky and still. Only thin peels of light-coloured clouds moved one behind the other, covering and uncovering the crispy crescent. We walked down the short stairs to the back yard. Bordered with plank walls, the backyard was a spacious setting with scrupulously trimmed bushes and with a tiny pond almost in the middle. Elina led me towards a big patio umbrella that was planted near to the pond. Under the umbrella sat three wicker chairs around a table.

"Have you ever had such experiences before…?" Elina probed worriedly as both of us settled into the chairs.

"No." I replied laconically, staring at the little fishes in that were swimming close to the bed of glossy pebbles that laid at the bottom of the pond.

"Like erratic mood swings, unstable self- images or abrupt outburst or any of that sort. Can you try to remember?" she sounded theatrical this time.

"I don't know". My voice quivered in dismay "I have no idea whatsoever it happening with me. But you know… the footsteps..." I whimpered shifting my glance from the pond to her face. Elina leaned forward toward me, her eyes looking for possible clues to complete the jigsaw that was presented to her.

"The Cliff, expanding moon, footsteps, turtle… a terrifying night mare!" I said summoning all my remaining energy.

"Tick… tick…tick…", I motioned the clock's moving needle wagging my fingers slowly. "I was waiting at the veranda, thirsty and tired. Everything around me felt silent except the tick of the clock which was clamped just above the window. I really don't know whether it was the silence that grew thicker or the tick of the clock that got louder, but in a short time I was completely drowned in a state of numbness. The next thing I knew, my mind was wandering aimlessly through a shady alleyway, narrowed with tall stone walls on either side, planked straight out to utter darkness. Soon, out of the blackness emerged the shadow of a turtle. All I could hear was the tramp of the turtle which merged perfectly with the tick of the clock. At once a bright flash blinded my eyes and when I regained my vision, we were trudging towards a cliff. All along our trek I could listen to a strange clucking sound that presumably set forth from the turtle's mouth. Eventually, for a moment, I gathered all my courage and peeked at the turtle's head. The uncanny creature was chewing something chunky and each time his jaws moved, a sort of dark sludgy liquid was oozing down his mouth. The sky was serene though, with umpteen stars and a big fat moon. But the serenity didn't stay long as I noticed an ominous expansion in the moon's size. It was ballooning at an alarming rate. It struck me like a lightening when I realised that the moon was actually plummeting towards earth for a big collision. A sort of compression overcame the whole of my body- a feeling as though each bit of my flesh was battling vigorously to rip off from my body and become thousands of different pieces. On the other hand, a certain binding force was struggling pathetically to hold them together as one body. Tormented by the painful conflict, I hurriedly looked at the turtle and placed my palm on my chest. All I could find on my chest was a sludgy pit. I quickly looked at the turtle and saw what it was chewing. My heart! Before I could open my mouth to scream, the moon, cliff, the turtle, all that was above and all that was beneath shattered to tiny bits" I propped my head against the head rest and heaved deep sigh.

"I see" said Elina tapping out a rhythm on the arm rest.

"Let it all hang out. Dreams are just..."
"Perhaps intuitions" I cut off Elina before she could finish her definition of dreams. "Maybe dreams are pointers towards something beyond our comprehension". "Maybe, maybe not" Elina replied "why worry too much of unnecessary things".
I extracted the crumpled magazine from my side pocket and tossed it over the table. Elina's was surprised at how I had

pocketed the magazine even in the middle such a mental turmoil. The magazine, as it flew to the table, unfolded itself, and landed on the table top revealing the turtle's picture. Elina peered at the creased front cover of the magazine. The turtle was still standing with its tear-filled eyes affixed to the sky.

"Are you saying you have an abstract connection with this magazine?" Elina investigated suspiciously.

"I might not be able to provide a satiable answer to that. Neither regarding the magazine nor the Con Man. All I know are indefinite episodes of events that deprives me of a peaceful sleep". I reached out for the cigarette case that Elina had laid on the table and lighted a cigarette. "I want you to know that Mann is a murderer. A cold- hearted brute". A gleaming drop of sweat blossomed and set forth from her hair, crawled down her forehead, did a swift run though her left cheek and finally detached from her face to her lap.

Chapter – 7
The Cliff: A New Fable

The breath of wind, as it dashed closely above the glassy lake forming ripples on its dark blue surface, caught sight of the stark ridges silhouetted against the glittering night sky. The dark- green turquoise veil of the sky appeared like a diaphanous membrane with orbs and brilliant, low hanging stars that moved constantly in a gaseous motion. Sparkling meteors swooped across the sky and vanished time and again. A waning gibbous, massive but irrelevant, floated between the celestial glitters. Bewitched by the pristine beauty of the mid- night sky, the wind manoeuvred a swift turn and climbed up the steep slope of the mountain, whizzing though the foliage.

Although the mountain cliff was refreshing enough to exhilarate the spirit of any living being, Evan- a wretched man, slouched against a large boulder, with teary eyes and withered face. He had become skin and bone within a week's time. His neck was scraggy and cheeks were shrunken. Two large childlike eyes sat in the sunken eye pits of his face. If it hadn't been for the scant strips of flesh that caught hold of his bones, he would have looked like a mobile skeleton. Raising his innocent eyes with effort, Evan swept the sky to spot the orange star which his wife always referred to as the star of companionship. After sometime of pursuit for the star he lowered his head as he felt intense strain in his neck and waited till the pain to subside so that he could start the search again. All the while he was straining his eyes, Evan could practically feel the throbbing pool of unshed tears in his temples that gave him an ugly head ache. His brittle hands wanted to caress their master's hair and console him but they couldn't find the courage to rise up and hence shivered in pity. Evan had eaten little since his wife's demise that had occurred almost a week before. From that day on he locked himself inside the house during the whole day and waited for the sun to fall, for the village roads to regain its stillness so that he could make a solitary trek to the cliff and spend the whole night looking for the orange gleam which he and his wife had enjoyed watching, even though they had seen it only three times in their entire life. When the mountainous villagers went to sleep under the secured guarding of mountains that surrounded their village, Evan frittered away the entire night at the forlorn peak, immersed in his solitude.

Evan and his wife appeared at the village two years back when they had learned about the mountains and the mesmerising view from its Cliff. Mysteries of the boundless sky and its magical existence always excited them and hence they were completely wallowed in sky watching. In his character, Evan was always a languid man, a day dreamer, who was always enmeshed in his fantastic world of thoughts. One would never see him chew the fat, for all the time he was mentally ruminating on his celestial findings. On the other hand, his wife was more pragmatic in her approach to life. Each morning, she would rise from her bed only after she apportioned her day hours according to her priorities. She was resolute and strong- willed unlike her dreamy companion. But, what she had lacked was Evan's remarkable sense of imagination. Evan was a pensive creature with very volatile emotional balance. Some days his frame of mind would pass through numerous rises and troughs within a short time span. But he found great respite in the warmth of his wife whenever despair befell him.

At the time when they moved in to the village as strangers, they invested most of their earnings in buying a portion of a manor from a wealthy village man. But now the manor was being taken care by his sons, Hani and Omar. Shortly after they settled, his wife joined the village primary school as a librarian where she spent the all her spare hours researching astronomy books. The husband and wife easily and quickly made a warm acquaintance with the twin brothers who were also fascinated in sky watching. Sooner the manor that they lived in became a clubbing spot for many other sky-watch enthusiasts who huddled up there by dusk and trekked together to the cliff for that day's observation.

At the cliff, a sizable flat rock that hung horizontally over cliff's edge provided ample footing for the crew and their instruments. They hung hammocks between the nearby trees for people to rest if anyone needed to. They got together at the manor at least four times a week and it was from there that they began their trek towards the cliff with their scopes and other instruments hung over their shoulders. But since the unfortunate occurrence of her death, the manor was barred to everyone; the door was opened only after the dusk and was closed before the first day light landed on earth. When back in the Manor after the night watch, Evan incarcerated himself inside the pale walls of high ceilinged bedroom where he was constantly tortured by the memories of his wife. Even though, Evan knew the miserable condition he was enduring, somewhere in the depth of his mind, he enjoyed the sweet pain of reliving through his dead wife's memories. Although his drooping eyelids and worn out body were begging him for a tranquil sleep, Evan dared not to because of the fear that a drowse might slump him into a terrible dream which would shatter him utterly. When abed he buried his head in the pillow, rich with the odour of his wife's hair. Pressing the pillow tightly to his head, Evan smothered himself trying to smell her hair.

Lovemaking, for Evan and his wife, was not only a bodily act but also a vehement exchange of passion where Evan found relief in unloading his entangled thoughts and his wife rejoiced in absorbing them. It was a morning after such a spirited night that Evan found his wife's soulless body lying aside him. A terrifying coldness, like Evan had never experienced before, had invaded her body. Her mouth was gaped open and was dark. Her eyes were glassy and still. Evan spent almost an hour, squeezing his head between his palms, puzzling over how life escaped her without his knowledge even though she was in his arms the whole night. Later that dusk, after his wife's funeral, Evan paced towards the cliff with long strides like a lunatic and spent the whole night staring at the prolific sky. These nocturnal visits of Evan, to the mountains, continued till the day when an unexpected stranger with all evil intentions emerged out of the darkness and enlightened him a path that, for him, was unknown till then.

Chapter – 8
The Guiding Light

Ascending the steep, the stream of wind arrived at the cliff, puffing and panting, and saw the desolated man behind the boulder. Skimming the wretched man tenderly and caringly, the wind moved past the trees and embarked on a tour to the adjacent ranges. For Evan the air had become thick and impregnated with his wife's odour. He inhaled a lungful of smell-infused air and held it in his lungs, wishing for it to spread all over his body. A decrepit owl that obscured in the rustling foliage, shook its furless head and screeched in fright as it's vicious watchful eyes caught sight of the stranger swaying in the hammock that was hung underneath. The stranger's large uncaring eyes were half closed and his willful face gleamed in the greenish – blue hue of the sky. With a vicious half smile, he upturned the hammock and landed on his feet. Behind him the strands of hammock twisted and tangled up like a cord. Frightened by the ominous air that surrounded the stranger, the owl flew off over his head with a chatter of its weak wings.

Through the corner of his eyes, Evan saw the peripheral vision of a shadowy figure walking towards him with crunch of dry leaves. But by the time he turned his head to see the figure, the stranger was already towering in front of him.

"How are you Evan?" the stranger enquired in his croaky yet caring voice. Evan's heart skipped a beat and he could do nothing but gape at the man from head to toe.

"Heard of your wife's passing. Devastated. are you?" The Stanger asked with a sympathetic smile. Evan didn't respond, all his attention was anchored at the stranger's chest that shook heavily as the man breathed in and out. His chest- hair bushed out through first two buttons that were left open. A long wiry beard concealed his healthy neck. The man squatted down right in front of Evan. Clasping Evan's chin the stranger brought his face in close proximity to Evan's face. The acrid stench of the man's breath and disrespectful invasion of private space irked Evan but he was too ensnared in the stranger's motionless eyes to put out his hands and push him away. For Evan, the stranger's dark brown eyeballs resembled the rim of a funnel through which glossy brown mud was cascading down to a pitch black, bottomless pit. From the inner corner of his eyes, set forth numerous nerves, thin and pink, and ramified throughout his eye.

"You must learn, Evan, that Sadness is most profound work of the omnipotent, the creator. Perhaps the last and the best. Without it how can man endure? without being in a constant tussle to rid one's woe, is it possible for one to make meaning of this whole deal" said the stranger and chortled. His breath lashed upon Evan's face like a gust.

The stressful stare down had tired Evan's eyes and his neck turned as feeble as a delicate straw that could not bear the weight of his head. Slowly as his head drooped, the stranger held him by his chin and lifted his head again.

"I am a dead man. how do I interest you in any manner?" Evan yelled shaking his head in an attempt to extricate his head from the stranger's clasp.

"Definitely not any of my concern. But how pitiful that you scorn yourself as a dead man. You would not say that if you have at least had a foretaste of its gleeful experience; timeless moment in which life breaks apart all its fetters and flows as pure energy". The Stanger laid on his back against the ground, gaped at the sky that had turned darker. A sparkling meteor leapt across the sky with its tail on fire.

"Watched it?" he asked Evan addressing the meteor "Have you watched a shooting star burn out and liberate itself from its confined form? It's just a teeny burning rock in the vast celestial space, but as it burns itself out, its existence becomes larger than the largest star. But if it happens to land on earth by any chance before it is reduced to ashes, the ill- fated rock would be condemned to live a perennial earthly life... Earthly life..." he giggled like a lunatic.

"You now Evan, I have, many times, risked a walk between life and death. But to my misfortune I was cursed to fall back to this mundane human loop again. This land is packed with bone heads. bone heads... bone heads..." he whimpered to himself.

"But I like you my friend" the stranger continued "The stranded man in you is what fascinates me and it strikes me like an intuition that you are one among the few who can understand my words. I admire you more because of your immense passion for the female who have just gone past the door of death" The stranger said flitting his eyes through the sky. "Don't you feel the damp wind Evan? Have you grown numb to the scent of human sweat? Aren't you feeling the warmth of her damp breath that has been caressing you every so often? It's your wife Evan. she has walked past the bridge and is now on the other side. Standing alone, she beckons you to join her for the eternal union. Do your knees possess enough strength to walk through the burning bridge to reach her? Are your senses still live to smell the sweet scent of death? I have had a foretaste of it".

"What? Taste of death?" Evan's eyes shone and he could not resist the urge to untangle the stranger's words. But he restrained himself from responding.

The stranger parted his lips, brought forth a bellow and recited like a poem.

Spurned into the womb as a seed of life

Rejected from the womb as a living piece of flesh

Tossed out of innocence and the spring of life

Is man not stumbling with the burden of thoughts

As he is being banished from one moment to the other

Till the final strike of his clock

The stranger bowed over the ground and riveted his eyes to the earth. The words that set forth from the stranger's lips transported Evan to a pensive mood.

"The final… joyous escape is not from your form but from the thoughts that gives you form, my friend" the stranger spoke again in a soft undulating voice looking at Evan.

"And at the verge, just when you are about to pass through the door of death, comes all the thoughts for a visit. In the beginning they intimidate you, winds up your nerves, overwhelms you with numbness and torments you by giving you the hardest hour you have ever been through. But gradually as you move further with firm steps, when your nerve unwinds, when blood rushes abundantly all through your body, and you feel as light as feather, the thoughts approach you for one last visit. But this time they beg you, implores you to not to forsake them and thereby the form they have created. And that moment strikes upon you with the revelation that the mortality is for the thoughts not your body; for your body longs to become free of any form and it is the thoughts that imposes an outline on it. That's the whole business of foretaste".

"Tell me more. Having instilled a seed of quest, you ought to explain more and enlighten me" Evan moved his lips and asked the stranger curiously and resolutely.

"What is beyond is unfathomable and hence inexplicable. All you get to know is the foretaste. After you bid farewell to your thoughts it is impossible to know its savour, for you have already become the savour" the stranger laid on his back and looked into the imponderable depth of the sky. "Like your wife I have also stood at the threshold, once. But I could not go beyond unlike her" as he spoke he raised his right arm, rolled up his sleeves till his elbow and rubbed his lower forearms on which a fat, discolored scar ran along its breadth. The dried up wound appeared like a disgusting hump on his tortured forearm. Evan curiously peered at the forearm and the dried up wound appeared to him like an ugly fat snail.

The disgusting appearance of the wound, his exhaustion and the thoughts of death gave Evan a strange feeling. Both terror and delight befell him at the same time. The air turned muggy and thick, and the odour of his wife invaded his nose still more. "She is here. With her moist tongue she is licking my mouth and face. Is she imploring me to rid myself of this dreadful flesh so that I may unite with her again and forever?" a pernicious suspicious caught Evan.

It was not just the stream of wind that watched over the two men talk, but also two other sky watchers who happened to be there; the twin brothers Hani and Omar. Standing off to one side of a big rooted tree, they overheard the uncanny conversation. And two days later, it was one of these twin brothers who, during his morning ride, caught sight of Evan's putrid and bloated body, floating on the dark blue lake.

That night Evan opened up to the stranger in a way he had never spoken to anyone before. He shared the immense mental pangs he had been enduring since his wife's departure, he told how he was being tormented by the teary swell on his temples and how he could not sleep. And the stranger, without uttering a word, listened to him attentively. On his face he mirrored perfectly, all the emotions that manifested on Evan's face. So precise was his mirroring that after a certain point it gave Evan a feeling that he was speaking to his own reflection. It was only when a pale orange hue seeped into the deep blue sky that they realized the long hours they had spent at the cliff, talking. Evan's eyes were tired, may be more tired than before. But when he descended the mountain with a foldable pocket knife that the new born friendship had bestowed him, a hue of determination shone brightly in his eyes.

Early morning at the embankment, just before the cocks had woken up to whistle off the day's drill, Evan delivered himself from the world which he considered miserable and began his journey to a world which he thought would be ecstatic. He slashed both his wrists and took a long bathe in the lake till the blue drew him down to her lap and sucked in all of his blood and tears. Sleep had finally approached him at blue bottom of the lake. The angel of sleep who had befallen him like a demon of nightmare had now visited him like a friendly angel. Evan closed his eyes under the water and waited for the foretaste to overcome him before he succumbed to a peaceful sopor.

Chapter – 9
The Beach House

The night was cold and breezy. Around ten o'clock, a sedan pulled up at the front gate. We were already back from the backyard and were sitting at the front room waiting for the taxi to arrive. We walked towards the street where the car, all heated up to gun to the beach house almost an hour away from Elina's residence, was waiting for us. After learning everything about Evan's incident, it was Elina who recommended that we go together to the one of her friend's beach house and spend a few days there and relax. I showed much excitement for the plan as I felt I was in need of some time off from all these hassles. The plan was as follows; me and Elina would journey together to the beach house where she would spend a day or two with me to help me acquaint to the place. Later she would return and will be paying weekly visits. Everything was planned at her discretion and all that had been planned sounded brilliant. We occupied both corners of the back seat and as soon as the doors were shut the car pulled off from the house. Swinging in and out through the curvy by-roads we finally hit the main road that planked straight out to the beach. Happy to find a plain empty road, the young exuberant driver got excited. Applying his leg weight slowly and softly on the accelerator he thoroughly enjoying the pace at which the car picked up speed.

Elina and me, like hopeless sailors stranded in an isolated island, looked out mindlessly at the roadside trees, lampposts and the never-ending guardrail that paraded past us and fell into our thoughts. I craned my neck out of the window to look at the sky but withdrew quickly as the wind was too powerful. For some reason, Elina was perturbed after she heard the incident at the cliff. And now, looking fixedly out of the window, the trees and lamp posts that whizzed by, she tried to subdue the bafflement and worry that manifested on her face. The window on my side after a certain point, opened up a different sight. On my side the trees and posts had vanished and only thing in my vision was the deep blue sky, vast boundless fields and a beautiful solitary star that hung in between. "If only I could be that star…" I reflected on myself as envy engulfed me.

I recollected an unreal, almost hallucinatory conversation that I once had with the sibyls who had told me that my existence was not different than a rat in a long narrow sewer. "One among those bristly rat who sustain themselves by chewing each other's furs and tails, and bred profusely" they had told me wagging their fingers.

"Live there… breed there… die there…" they had cursed. In my imagination, the condition of the sewer was still more miserable, even though the visitations never revealed them; narrow slimy walls, turd – reeking air and the hungry new born pups who bit anything and everything, thinking that all that they bit and chewed were milk secreting breasts.

They really made me believe I was a rat, a dreadful creature in a long sewage tunnel. But what the sibyls did not say and what I saw was the light of hope that gleamed at the far end of the sewer. For some unknown reason the tiny dot of light evoked hope in me.

"With all my might… with all my might… towards the light" I murmured and clutched my fist. The dreadful state of mind that I was in, was at once stirred by the touch of Elina's soft fingers. Slowly I felt her warm fingers swallow my fist.

The comforting embrace of her fingers slacked my clench. Turning my head half way around, I looked at Elina. Moment to moment, her face lit up and shadowed out under the light of the street lamp that passed by. Shortly, the rumble of the waves, as it crashed against the rocky shore, was heard from a distance even before the sea came to sight. The air turned soupy and salty. As the driver saw the resort house, that perched on a little mount close to the shore, facing the sea, he drifted out from the main road and took the bumpy sandy path that led to the destination. As we reached in front of the lobby, an enormous, neck-less man with his huge paunch overhanging his belt, waddled towards our car. Placing the full weight of his mammoth arms on the lowered window, as if trying to tip the car over, he bent forward and placed his large face squarely towards my face. I regarded the interesting features of the mammoth man. His thick and black moustache poured over his lips. His eyes were large and his pudgy scraped cheeks were wobbling as he spoke. He spoke to Elina breathing the stench of alcohol heavily my face.

"Welcome Madam. Boss had called up to arrange for your visit" guest- manager greeted Elina in his croaky voice, ruling me out completely from the scene.

"Lucky that its off season. Otherwise we are always booked. As soon as I received the call, I've ordered the boys to arrange the best room we have. the best room, the best..." the colossus tried to please Elina with a simper which looked whimsical and disgusting for his weather- beaten face. While he spoke Elina dug out a sheaf of currency and peeled out four bills to the driver and he happily returned a grateful simple. We both alighted from the car and followed the colossus one behind another through a single-loaded corridor. Just when we were about to reach the corridor's end, the colossus shoved his plump fist into his pocket and unearthed a key which seemed so weeny for his huge plump palms. He tickled the door with the key and it opened with a sheepish howl. The inside of the small room was stuffed tightly with too many furniture; a floor bed that consumed more than half the space, a tiny table with a dusty surface and a stool underneath, a wilted indoor plant on one side of the bed and next to it a mini refrigerator. The whole room was richly lighted with amber glow that cascaded from the bright electric lantern that hung from the ceiling like a pendent. One wall of the room, near the foot of the bed, was draped with shabby black cloth, behind which stood the glass doors to the balcony.

"Good?" asked the colossus with the simper crippling his face.

"Good enough" replied Elina, chuckling at his efforts to appear responsible. She turned towards me and said she will be back soon and disappeared with the man. Threading my way through the furniture I parted the drapes and opened the balcony door. The sight from the balcony was that of a serene shore with big round boulders on which frothy waves crashed alternately. The endless sea that shimmered in the milky light of the moon refreshed my eyes. Leaving the door open I reclined on the bed with my back against its headboard and took out the magazine from my pocket. I held it over my head, gazed at the face page and found the turtle gloomier under the darkness of the amber light that fell from the lantern. Elina's footsteps reached my ears. I quickly shut the magazine, tossed it over to the table and watched it land flat on the table top with the turtle side down. Exactly at that moment, Elina appeared at the doorway. She methodically walked inside and bolted the door, drew the stool and sat down on it, all in an unbroken chain of action.

"I must thank you my love, such a pleasant place. Such a serene air. Everything would have been so at peace of it wasn't for the... the Mann, who still..." I said and shifted my position for assuming a serious mood.

"Don't be worried. We are on the right track" although she tried to reassure me she felt it wasn't fair to deprive me of truth anymore and said this. "Well... To be honest, it seems enigmatic. But I can definitely say that it's going to end well. But right now what I want you to do is to conduct me through some more of your past." she said in an authoritative yet affectionate tone.

"Of course" I replied instantly "you have the liberty to ask anything, anything". Even though my voice was overflowing with confidence and trust, I reckon, Elina didn't have the same trust in me, because last time when she had pressed a sensitive button she had saw me turning into a manic.

"Alright that's perfect" said Elina in her usual gentle voice.

"I want to ask you dear, why does Evan's suicide burden you so much? Many times I saw your eyes welled up with tears when you were explaining his story. Was he a friend or what was he for you to have such an emotional downfall due to his death?" she asked with a pause between each word so as to make it as clear as possible. "And I completely understand if these questions give you a bad taste and in that case I don't want you to dig into things that bother you. Otherwise, just try to recall how all these happenings were revealed to you and when you met all these people" Elina said and fell silent.

For almost a minute that ensued, we sat quiet. Moment after moment, silence swelled up like a balloon and just when it reached a point where it could not grow anymore, I burst it out with the honed words that somehow came to me instinctively.

"I haven't seen any of them" I said and watched the expressions that played on Elina's charming face. "Not Evan, nor Mr. Mann or Mrs. Chloe. I cannot recall ever having seen them personally because I simply haven't seen them". As soon as I finished, I observed in Elina, an expression, neither astonishment nor bewilderment but a sense of achievement that flushed her face.

I went on "Everything, I know about them are through stories and songs which I learned from the old Sibyls that comes to meet me very often. But from further probe and from the changes that happened in and around me post those events, I am sure that the stories were not just stories but real incidents."

"The old Sibyls!?" asked Elina with an unrestrained curiosity. Elina, as I remember, was a person who was much intrigued by the tales and stories of mystical seers, fortune tellers and other other-worldly creatures and we have had day-long conversations on these subjects in our past.

"Yes, the old Sibyls" I said in a low voice, almost like a whisper. "Two identical sibyls with humped back and protruding eyes come often and thud on my door. Every time I heard their thunderous bang on the door, my teeth chattered feverishly. And when I eventually open the door after a long grapple with my fear, the sibyls would be standing in front of the door, with their dilapidated body rocking in tune with their loud guffaw that revealed their slimy and broken teeth. The half- naked oldies had their wrinkled skin sagging off the bones. The thin strands of their grey hair were gathered and twirled up into a bun on top of their visible skull. Heavy earrings hung down their ear lobes forming a big hollow".

My eyes danced around and my hands motioned involuntarily as I tried to word the image of sibyls.
"Where do you meet these sibyls?" Elina peered at me doubtfully with more curiosity.

"In my sleep" I said immediately. "Sometimes it is during a nice cozy sleep that they come thudding on the door. During the recent visit, one of the Sibyls had brought a turtle, leading it by a wicker cord. A strange occurrence of which I didn't know what to make of, and the docile turtle, perhaps victim of her conjuration, was licking her shrunken feet". Elina nodded lightly as she realized the reason why I was engrossed in the magazine.

"Whenever the sibyls entered, they would squat down on either side of my bed and in a torn out voice they would tell me all these incidents about Mann, Hide, Evan and so on. They would tell these tales so eloquently that I, like a child, would sit and listen to their stories without a wink. Sometimes they chant their uncanny spells, sprinkle a handful of ash and bewitch me to live the characters of their tales. Eventually they would wag their bark-like fingers and torment me saying that I was to blame for all the bad that happened. All I could do was to succumb to their harassment like a mute listener and weep inside. And at the end of each visit they would taunt me with a giggle and wish me good sleep before they wobbled out through the door. Upon further probe, I found out that all the characters of their tales were real living people and those occurrences were shockingly true. Little by little, regret took root inside me as I started feeling this strange self- contempt. And each time the sibyls visited, their menacing words and scorn swelled up my self-pity and regret".

"Crazy man… crazy…" Elina heaved a sigh and ran her fingers over her hair. She rose from the stool and moved towards the mini- refrigerator. "Would you mind having a beer?" she asked me as she opened the door and grabbed two beer cans and threw one to the bed. Drawing the pull ring of the can with a fizz, she mouthed a long gulp. "Crazy man… you" she tilted her head with a smile. She came in front of me, placed her beautiful fingers on my head, stroked my hair for a while and brought my head towards her middle. I listened to the thumps of her heart. The next thing I know; we were frolicking in the bed, entwined in each other's arms.

Elina straddled across my loins and teased me with blissful gallops. Her cheeks turned scarlet as she blushed and laughed. In her eyes gleamed an excitement as thought she was riding off to an other- worldly shore. Perhaps, she might have ridden vehemently towards the Dali's shore of 'Melting Clocks'; the blissful shore where the clocks lay melted, turning everything mortal to immortal. However, for Elina, exactly at that blessed moment when she sets foot on the blissful shore, the shore itself will cease to exist; because the clocks in the real world where she and I belong are solid. I impulsively felt an irresistible desire to be there at the shore with her and listen to the ecstatic giggle of the earth as waves licked her belly. I gently closed my eyes and I was there.

Chapter – 10
The Last Day - Break

The next day, callow warmth of the morning sun seeped in though thc slits of the drape and fell obliquely on my face. Wishing to remain in the comfort of the pleasant sleep, I closed my eyes and felt for Elina who had slept beside me. But she had already left the place. "Where has she left?" I pondered as I walked towards the balcony. Parting the drape, I slid in to the narrow balcony which had enough room only for one chair. Before my eyes, the picturesque sea laid aback like a lascivious female. Her torso, covered in blue veil rippled as the wind blew his warm breath. Her bosoms swelled as he skimmed her with his tender fingers and her moan reached my ears like a hum. I sat at the balcony enjoying the sight.

"Excuse me" came the croaky voice of the guest manager. I made my way through the furniture, opened the door and found the colossus standing with a mug of coffee in one hand and a wheat-colored envelop in the other.

"Here is your coffee. We have the best eatery" he said as he gave me the cup and smiled.

"And this" he said waving the envelop "letter is for you. Elina strictly told me to personally hand it to you once you wake up" he said with the same simper.

"Thank you" I took the letter from his hand.

"Did Elina say anything else?... regarding any journey or something?" I enquired.

"Nothing. But she said she will be back today or latest by tomorrow morning. Allow me to leave, I have to supervise the refurbishing work at our new lounge. If you need something, ring the reception" said the huge man and strode away hurriedly.

Opening the envelop, I found a white four-folded paper. "Where did Elina go? How strange that she chose to write?". Unfolding the letter as quickly as possible, I sank to the bed and began to read.

"Dear,

I am on my way to Evan's village. I intend to speak with Hani and Omar about the incident.

Pardon me if this is not the proper way to communicate what I am about to say. But, learning it through the letter would give you enough time to reconcile with the reality. Understand that Mr. Mann is just a hollow name. An imaginary man or perhaps even a title you for picked up for your confession. However, it would be imprudent to believe that it's a random name. It might possibly have its own genesis which we shall probe into later. I am looking forward to discussing your preternatural experiences. All what you need to do right now is relax. I hope the brothers would understand your situation and be convinced enough to withdraw their accusation. I will meet you soon".

To have everything fall into its place, precisely and exactly where you want it, is a such an unparalleled feel. It has always brought a triumphant smirk on my face. But now, in the depth of my mind, beyond the exhalation of a win there lurked something that was stirring and made me ponder.

I crumpled the letter, threw it to the floor and walked alongside the bed, towards glass door. I stood there gazing at the sea and in an unforeseen moment, a pod of dolphins bound high up in the air one after the other and plopped backed into the Sea's womb. One of them, perhaps her most beloved daughter, had a human head and the lean voluptuous body of a fish. Before my eyes she appeared like a mermaid.

For some unknown reason, the image of the turtle flashed in my mind. I went to the table, drew the stool and sat upright on it with the magazine in my arms. I gazed at the turtle. It was still desolate, pensive and pleading. Thumbing gently through the first two pages I reached the third page where a fable was printed. Each word of the fable; the turtle, heavenly ocean, labyrinth, mirror maze, curse, rebirth, revelation…, for some reason, felt like a rusty iron chain and I was enchained in it. For a brief moment, existence seemed awkward and embarrassing. And before long, there came a moment where I felt empty and fresh like a new born. The first words came wafting and gliding to my empty mind.

"Like the furious blaze that wakes up mirage; behind every illusion lurks its secreted truth. The illusion that Man is many and the truth that he is none"

And with a cold shudder streaming down my spine I looked at the authors name and it read 'Mann'.

www.ingramcontent.com/pod-product-compliance
Lightning Source LLC
LaVergne TN
LVHW092024190726
843493LV00002B/576